Full Moon

Written by Ellen Weisberg and Ken Yoffe
Illustrated by Kira Gousios

It was Halloween night. Cold night winds blew against the mask that covered my face. I looked up at the huge maple tree in front of my family's home and could see the large, pale October moon behind it.

I heard my older sister, Amy, still inside the house, in the front parlor.

"Okay," Amy said. "Let's go."

I grabbed hold of the edge of my sister's sweater with one hand. With the other, I swung a plastic container shaped like a gutted pumpkin. Ghosts and goblins and witches passed us by. Each one stumbled along in big, baggy costumes. I saw one or two reach below their hot masks to scratch their cheeks. I smiled as I danced among them.

"Amy?" I asked.

"Uh-huh?"

"I heard there's a man who lives on the moon."

"Did you," Amy said. She had been only half listening to me. She was also making sure to tightly hold my hand so we could safely cross the street.

"I also heard that the moon is made of cheese," I said. I tried to keep up with my sister's quick pace. "Doesn't the cheese get moldy, being outside for so long?"

"I guess so," Amy said distantly. She tried to see if the porch light of a neighbor's house was on or off.

"And wouldn't the man who lives on the moon get tired of eating moldy cheese all the time?" I asked. As I continued to walk, my smile started to fade. I stared up at the bright round ball in the black sky. If there really was a man living on the moon, then how he could sleep with all that blinding light? Maybe he was being kept awake for days on end, and his tiredness made him clumsy. Maybe he'd occasionally trip and fall into one of the many huge holes I had heard were on the moon.

My head was still turned up
toward the sky when Amy and
I approached a lit doorway.
A woman greeted us, holding a
large dish loaded with gold- and
silver-wrapped chocolates.
I grabbed a handful and smiled
quickly up at her. I dropped my
treats into my plastic pumpkin.
I then turned again toward the
cold, autumn night sky.

Later that night, I dumped colorful lollipops onto the center of my bed. Bite-sized bars of milk and dark chocolate followed, and so did liquid-filled wax sticks and packets of watermelon- and strawberry-flavored bubble gum. I stared down at my Halloween collection. My mouth began to water.

Then I started to think about the man on the moon.

The poor little man on the moon.

I stood up and walked over to my sister's desk. I picked up a pad of paper and tried to spell words out on it with a sharpened pencil.

Dear men who go to the moon,

Here is candy for the man
who lives there.
I don't want him to eat anymore
moldy cheese. Also please give
him my witch's mask.
It will keep the light out when
he goes to sleep.
Thank you.
Jessica

I opened the top drawer of Amy's desk. I pulled out a large, tan envelope. I flipped it over and started to write as neatly and carefully as I could.

From: Jessica
At Jessica's home

To: Men Who Go To The Moon
At The Place Where There Are Rockets

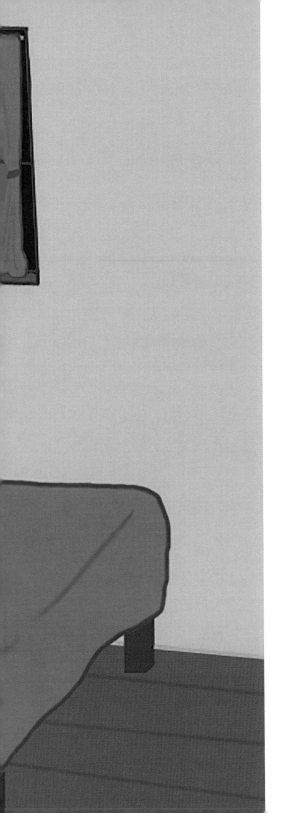

I stared down at the envelope. Would the postman understand where I wanted my letter to go? I scratched the side of my head. Of *course* he'd know where to bring my letter. *Everybody* knew where rockets were launched. I lifted the envelope up and blew some eraser shavings off of it.

I carried it over to my bed and started to shove as many candies as would fit inside of it. I then took my witch's mask and also placed it inside, just barely getting it to fit.

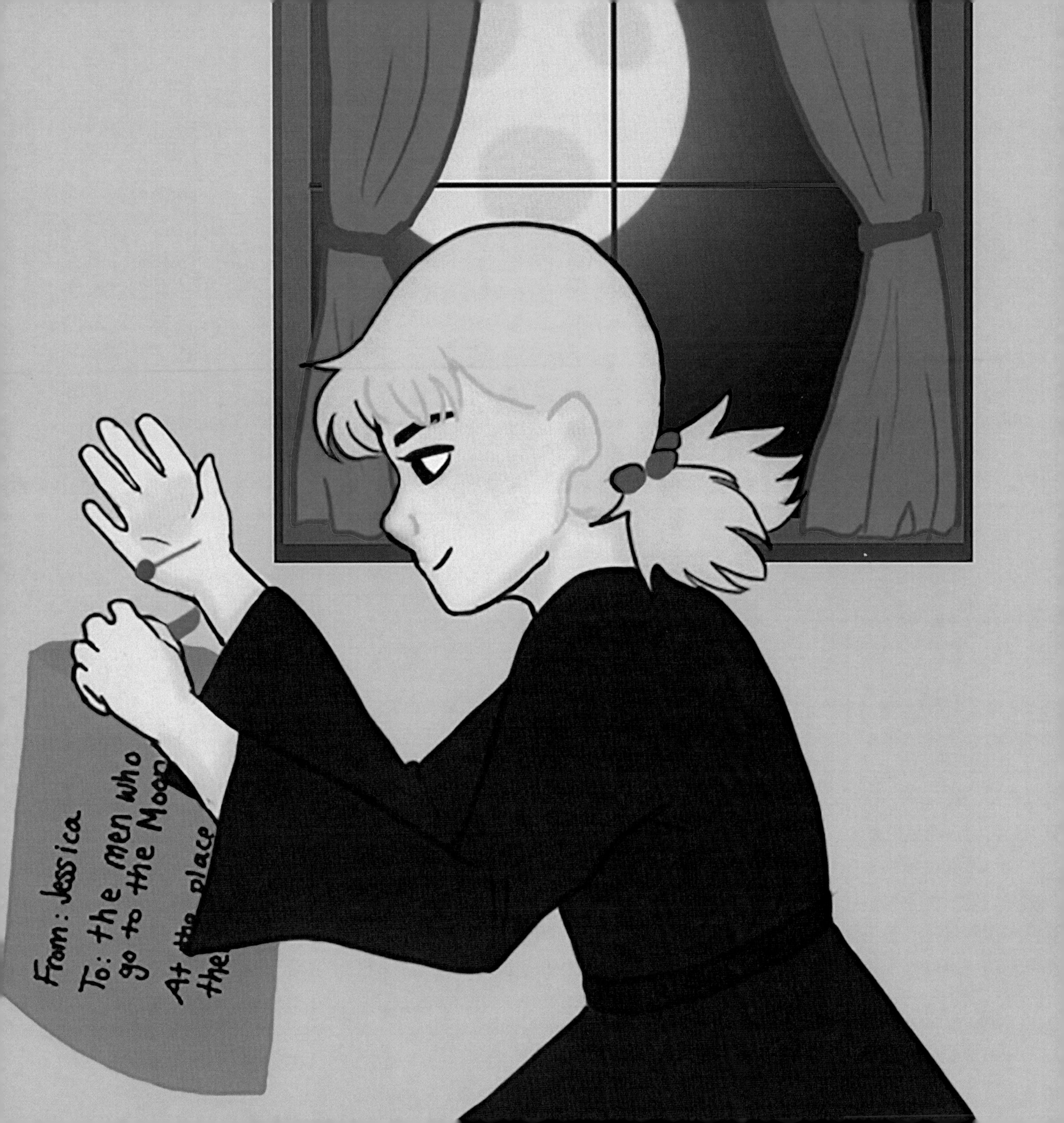
From: Jessica
To: the men who
go to the Moon

My care package was ready to go. I carried it out to the mailbox. I shoved the envelope inside and closed the mailbox lid. I raised a rusty red, metal flag up. I'd seen my mother do this to tell the postman that there was something there for him to take away. I turned on one heel and walked back toward the house.

It was a cold, early November night. I sat upright in my bed and grabbed the edges of my blanket. I brought it to my chin. I tried to catch a glimpse of the moon outside my window, but a thick mist had drifted across the sky. It hid each and every sparkling and glittering thing that was behind it. I sighed loudly and placed my head in my hands. I found myself thinking again about the man on the moon.

The poor man on the moon.

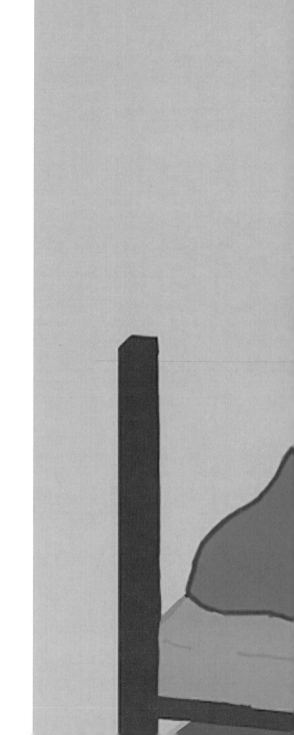

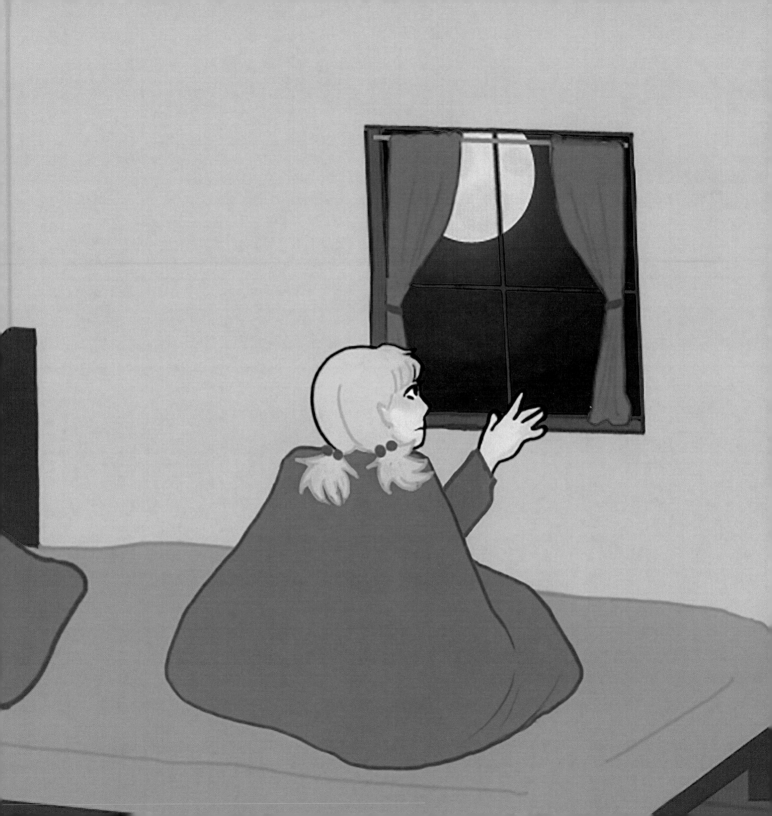

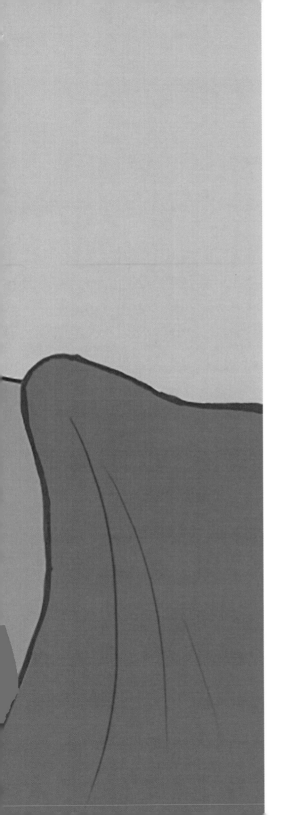

I reached behind my head to fluff my pillow. I pressed its sides close together and made its center thick and full. Then I noticed a tiny envelope peeking out from underneath it. I picked it up and read the words "To Jessica" on the outside.

It couldn't have been money from the tooth fairy because I hadn't lost any new teeth. It couldn't have been a gift from Santa Claus because Christmas wasn't for another month. I excitedly opened the envelope's seal and pulled out a piece of stationary.

"Dear Jessica," the note read. "Thank you for your kindness. Your friend, The Man on the Moon."

My heart was pounding.
I stared at the note. The man on the moon dotted his eyes just like my sister Amy did. He drew his "y's" and his "e's" the same as she did, too!

I flung my covers off. I leapt out of bed and raced toward the window. There was a small clearing in the sky, where I could just barely see a fuzzy glow of pale, yellow light. I smiled a wide smile.

To me, the moon had never looked friendlier, or fuller.

FACEPAINT Nonprofit Books

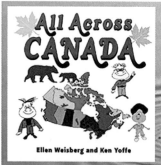

All Across CANADA

Ellen Weisberg and Ken Yoffe

All Across **EUROPE**

Ellen Weisberg and Ken Yoffe

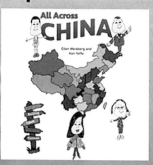

All Across **CHINA**

Ellen Weisberg and Ken Yoffe

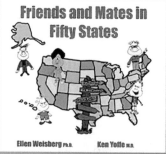

Friends and Mates in Fifty States

Ellen Weisberg Ph.D.   Ken Yoffe M.D.

Angel Rock Leap

Ellen Weisberg
Ken Yoffe

What are microscopes?

ELLEN WEISBERG AND KEN YOFFE

Full MOON

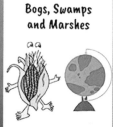

Bogs, Swamps and Marshes

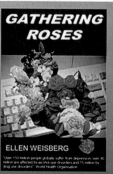

GATHERING ROSES

ELLEN WEISBERG

https://facepaint.team

Fruit of the Vine

Ellen Weisberg & Ken Yoffe

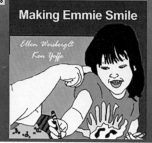

Making Emmie Smile

Ellen Weisberg & Ken Yoffe

FACEPAINT Nonprofit's multi-award-winning anti-bullying
3D animation, Justin and the Werloobee!

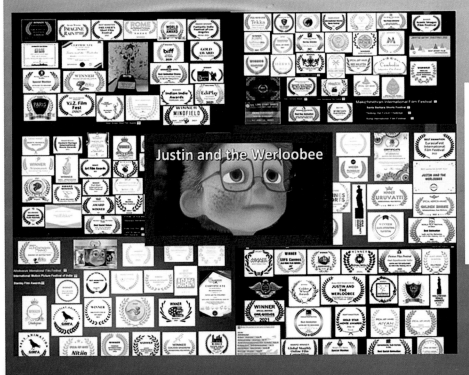

Watch on YouTube!

Made in United States
North Haven, CT
24 October 2022

25847621R00018